Contents

JOHN GALSWORTHY

The Man of Property

Retold by Margaret Tarner

HEINEMANN

UPPER LEVEL

Series Editor: John Milne

The Heinemann Guided Readers provide a choice of enjoyable reading material for learners of English. The Series is published at five levels – Starter, Beginner, Elementary, Intermediate and Upper. Readers at **Upper Level** are intended as an aid to students which will start them on the road to reading unsimplified books in the whole range of English literature. At the same time, the content and language of the Readers at **Upper Level** is carefully controlled with the following main features:

Information Control

As at other levels in the series, information which is vital to the development of a story is carefully presented in the text and then reinforced through the Points for Understanding section. Some background references may be unfamiliar to students, but these are explained in the text and in notes in the Glossary. Care is taken with pronoun reference.

Structure Control

Students can expect to meet those structures covered in any basic English course. Particularly difficult structures, such as complex nominal groups and embedded clauses, are used sparingly. Clauses and phrases within sentences are carefully balanced and sentence length is limited to a maximum of four clauses in nearly all cases.

Vocabulary Control

At **Upper Level**, there is a basic vocabulary of approximately 2,200 basic words. At the same time, students are given the opportunity to meet new words, including some simple idiomatic and figurative English usages which are clearly explained in the Glossary.

Glossary

The Glossary at the back of this book on page 89 is divided into 4 sections. A number beside a word in the text, like this [3], refers to a section of the Glossary. The words within each section are listed in alphabetical order. The page number beside a word in the Glossary refers to its first occurrence in the text.

A Note About The Author

John Galsworthy was born in Surrey, England on 14th August, 1867. The Galsworthys were rich and shortly after he was born, the family moved into a fine house on a very large estate in Coombe, in Surrey. It was this home that Galsworthy was thinking about when he wrote about Robin Hill in his story, *The Forsyte Saga*.

When he was 14, Galsworthy went to Harrow, the famous boys' school. Five years later, he went to New College, Oxford to study Law. However, he was not a particularly clever student – he preferred to watch horse-racing!

Galsworthy passed his exams but did not do much law work. In 1895, Galsworthy had met and fallen in love with a singing teacher, Sybil Carr. His family did not approve of this young woman and so they had sent him abroad. He travelled to

Canada, the Caribbean and Russia.

John Galsworthy married his wife, Ada, in 1905. She and Galsworthy had met ten years earlier at a family party to cele-brate Ada's marriage to Galsworthy's cousin, Arthur. Ada and Arthur's marriage was very unhappy. Galsworthy heard about Ada's troubles and they began to meet secretly. When people found out about Ada and John they were shocked. The lovers were not accepted by fashionable society.

Both his brother-in-law, the painter George Sauter, and Ada encouraged Galsworthy to write. For eleven years he did not earn any money. But in 1906, Galsworthy wrote *The Man of Property* and it was a great success. People thought it told the story of Ada and her unhappy marriage to Arthur.

Galsworthy wrote books, plays, articles and letters. (See the list at the back of this book.) He was very interested and concerned about many political and social issues.

In 1910, Galsworthy met a young dancer, Margaret Morris. Margaret was 19 and John was 43. She was acting in his play, *The Little Dream*. Ada did not say anything when she found out that her husband was in love with the young woman. Galsworthy finally decided to try and forget Margaret and he and Ada went abroad.

Galsworthy was unable to fight in the First World War (1914–18). He was too old. Instead he worked in a hospital in France. Later he gave his house in England to be used as a hospital for wounded soldiers.

Galsworthy was given honorary degrees from Princeton and Dublin universities. In 1926, Galsworthy bought a large house in Sussex. By then he was a famous writer and a rich 'man of property'.

Galsworthy was given the Nobel Prize for Literature in 1932. He died on 31st January, 1933 after six months' of illness. He was 65 years old.

A Note About England in the Nineteenth Century

In England in the nineteenth century, most upper-class people who had certain ideas about behaviour were part of 'polite society'. People in polite society had fixed ideas about what they should wear, where they should go and what kind of music, painting, etc., they should like.

Most of the people in polite society were wealthy. But it was not enough just to be wealthy. A wealthy man in polite society had to own things like land, horses and paintings.

In the nineteenth century, a woman was not able to own anything when she married. All her property belonged to her husband. And some husbands thought of their wives only as another piece of property.

The Forsytes are an example of an upper-class family in polite society. They are wealthy, own fine houses and collect valuable china and paintings. And they also know how to behave politely to one another and to others. They are 'respectable' – the adjective used by polite society to describe what they thought was correct.

The People in This Story

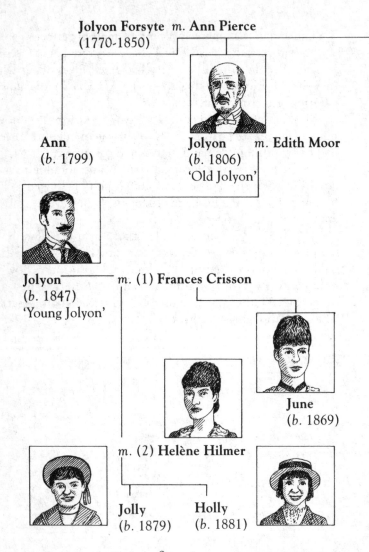

Jolyon Forsyte *m.* **Ann Pierce**
(1770-1850)

Ann
(*b.* 1799)

Jolyon *m.* **Edith Moor**
(*b.* 1806)
'Old Jolyon'

Jolyon — *m.* (1) **Frances Crisson**
(*b.* 1847)
'Young Jolyon'

June
(*b.* 1869)

m. (2) **Helène Hilmer**

Jolly   **Holly**
(*b.* 1879)   (*b.* 1881)

FORSYTE FAMILY TREE

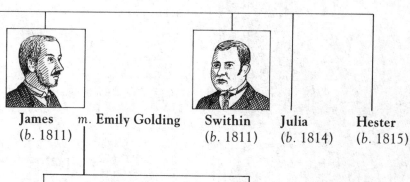

James *m.* **Emily Golding**
(*b.* 1811)

Swithin
(*b.* 1811)

Julia
(*b.* 1814)

Hester
(*b.* 1815)

Soames *m.* **Irene Heron**
(*b.* 1855

Winifred *m.* **Montague Dartie**
(*b.* 1858)

Philip Bosinney

1

The Forsytes meet Philip Bosinney

June 15th, 1886, was an important day for the Forsyte family. It was a day they would always remember. For the first time in twelve years, Old Jolyon Forsyte, the head of the family, was giving an afternoon party in his great house at Stanhope Gate. The party was to celebrate the engagement[1] of Old Jolyon's grand-daughter, June, to Mr Philip Bosinney.

The day was important for a different reason too. Philip Bosinney, the man who planned to marry June Forsyte, was going to change the lives of many people in the Forsyte family.

It was four o'clock in the afternoon of that June day in 1886. Many carriages[1] were making their way to the house where Old Jolyon had lived for so many years. Stanhope Gate was a wealthy and respectable[1] part of London and Old Jolyon's house was one of the biggest in the district. High steps led up to the front door and the tall house seemed to look down on passers-by. Such a house made Old Jolyon's position in the world quite clear. Only a man of the greatest wealth could afford to live there.

All the Forsytes lived in London at that time, and they were all people of wealth and good taste[1]. They lived in fine-looking houses which they had filled with beautiful and expensive things. The Forsytes were collectors; they liked to own property of all kinds. Money was important to them for this reason. With money, they could buy houses, old paintings and fine china. They could dress in the most fashionable clothes[1].

The Forsytes looked very fine as they stepped down from their carriages and went into Old Jolyon's house. They walked slowly up the stairs to the drawing-room.

It was a large drawing-room, usually dark and gloomy, but today it looked different. The light colours of the womens' summer dresses brightened the dark walls and heavy furniture. The room was filled with the sound of voices making polite conversation[1]. The younger members of the family moved from group to group. The older Forsytes sat upright on hard chairs or stood against the walls. They were thinking of other family parties that had been given in this room many years before.

Today, the Forsytes seemed even more confident[4] and dressed more finely than usual. There was a reason for this. As a family, they felt danger. Of course, Forsyte girls had got married before and some of them had married poor men. But the Forsytes felt that Philip Bosinney was very different from themselves. And because he was different, they did not trust him. They all knew that June was Old Jolyon's grand-daughter who would one day be a very rich woman.

Who was this Philip Bosinney? Was he a rich man? No, certainly not. He was a poor architect who did not even own a house. He lived in one untidy room behind his office. Some people said Bosinney was a clever architect who would one day be a successful man. The houses he designed were unusual and in good taste. One day these houses might be worth a lot of money, but Bosinney did not seem to care about that. He had no respect for property[1].

One of the young Forsytes had called Philip Bosinney 'The Buccaneer'. The name was a clever one and now most of the Forsytes used it. A buccaneer was a kind of pirate, a man who took away other people's property. A buccaneer lived boldly and carelessly.

Perhaps the Forsytes were right to be worried. Certainly, strange stories were told about this young man. Bosinney dressed strangely too, more like an artist than a respectable man of business. Some of the Forsytes were artistic themselves; one of them painted and one wrote pretty pieces of music. But all the Forsytes knew how to dress and how to behave well.

The Forsytes walked slowly round the large drawing-room, talking quietly to each other and looking across to where Bosinney stood. He was certainly wearing odd clothes and there was something unusual about his face too. It was bony and thin and his hair was curly and rather untidy. Bosinney's brown eyes shone strangely as he glanced round the room from one Forsyte to another. There was a small smile on his face.

Old Jolyon was glad to see the room full of people. It reminded him of the old days. He and June lived alone in the big house now and June would be leaving it when she married. Old Jolyon found it hard to believe that June was engaged. He still thought of her as a little child.

Old Jolyon was not very happy about June's engagement to Bosinney, but the old man was too proud to show his feelings. June had many strange friends, most of them poor. Bosinney did not care about money but that did not worry Old Jolyon too much. Old Jolyon was much more worried because he believed that the young man did not really love June enough. It was for this reason that Old Jolyon had refused to let June and Bosinney marry until at least one year had passed.

2

Philip Bossiney Meets Irene

Old Jolyon looked around the room in which the party was being held. It was a room that he had known for so many years. It was dark and the furniture was heavy, but it was the room of a man with a great deal of money and good taste. The walls were covered with valuable old paintings and along the walls were several large cupboards with glass doors. They were

The Forsytes walked slowly round looking across to where Bosinney stood.

full of valuable pieces of china painted in rich colours.

James Forsyte, Old Jolyon's brother, stood by one of these cupboards, holding a beautiful piece of china. He was turning it over and over in his hands, trying to guess how much Old Jolyon had paid for it. James was very tall and thin and he was carefully and correctly dressed. Everything he ever did was done correctly and carefully. He was, of course, a rich man and he owned several houses, but spending money made him feel unhappy and afraid. He never did anything without a great deal of careful thought.

Near James, leaning against the piano, was James' twin brother, Swithin. Swithin was tall too, but he was fat and heavy. Swithin was not married and he liked to spend his money on food, wine and fine clothes. He always wore high stiff collars because he thought they were fashionable. Today his collar was so high that he could hardly move his head. Swithin was also wearing two fine waistcoats, one of them was bright red and had gold buttons.

Old Jolyon looked at his brothers for a minute and then turned his head slightly to look at his grand-daughter, June. Like her grandfather, June was standing very straight. She was small and slim with a great deal of bright red hair.

June was not beautiful, but her red hair and blue eyes made her look interesting. She always said what she thought and, like her grandfather, she was very stubborn[4].

June was standing close to Philip Bosinney as though she was trying to protect him from her family. June felt that she and Bosinney were being inspected and she did not like that at all.

One by one, the Forsytes came up to Bosinney. They looked at him carefully, smiled, and then walked slowly away. June went on talking to Bosinney, but he did not really listen to what she was saying. His light brown eyes glanced round the room from one person to another. Bosinney showed no interest in anyone until he noticed a tall, beautifully-dressed woman standing by herself.

This woman was standing very still and yet she seemed to move gently like a flower in the wind. Although she said very little, everyone in the room looked at her. The women looked at her perfect clothes, but the men looked at her soft, golden hair and large, dark eyes.

Bosinney stared at this woman as a man looks at a beautiful picture. Then he turned quickly to June and said, 'Who is that woman? Please introduce me to her.'

June was very happy. Smiling with pleasure, she took Philip Bosinney up to the tall, graceful woman.

'This is Irene,' June said. 'She is my best friend, Phil. Please be good friends, you two.'

All three smiled at each other and began to talk. Another man came up to them silently and stood beside the beautiful Irene. He stood beside her as though she was his property. This was Soames Forsyte, Irene's husband.

Soames and Philip Bosinney looked at each other carefully. They were completely different in every way. Soames, like his father, James, was a solicitor and a business man. Bosinney was an architect, almost a kind of artist. Soames had always disliked June and now he felt that he disliked Bosinney too. But these four people were part of polite society. So they smiled at each other and spoke as though they were all friends.

'You and Philip must have dinner with us, June,' said Irene in her soft voice.

'Of course you must,' said Soames.

Irene turned to look at her husband as she spoke. The smile that had been on her face died away.

All the Forsytes had noticed that Irene never smiled at her husband. Many of them had guessed that Soames and Irene were not happy together. But, as a family, they pretended not to notice. Old Jolyon had once called his nephew, Soames, 'the Man of Property[1]'. The name was not meant to please Soames.

16

*Bosinney noticed a tall, beautifully-dressed woman
standing by herself.*

Old Jolyon did not like him, even though Soames was the son of Old Jolyon's brother, James. Soames, more than any other Forsyte, loved to own property, especially things of beauty.

When Soames had met Irene a few years before, he had had a great desire to make her his wife. At that time, Irene had been living with her father, an extremely poor man. Soames did his best to make Irene love him. He gave her many presents and asked her to marry him, time after time.

While her father was alive, Irene was strong enough to refuse Soames. But after her father's death, Irene was left alone. Soames continued to see her whenever he could and at last she agreed to marry him. She did not love him, but everyone thought it was a good marriage. Soames had money and Irene had beauty. What could be better?

Soames was proud to be seen with his lovely and intelligent wife. She had become his most valuable piece of property. But Irene hated her husband and they had very little to say to each other. More than anything else, Irene wanted to leave Soames, but of course he refused to give up his property. The marriage was a failure.

At last, people started to leave the drawing-room. Everybody had stayed for the correct amount of time[1]. One by one, the Forsytes said goodbye to Old Jolyon, shook hands with June and took one last look at Philip Bosinney before they went. The inspection was over.

3

A Lonely Old Man

The following day, Old Jolyon was sitting alone in his gloomy study. The old man was tired and he had fallen asleep while he was reading the newspaper. Suddenly he woke up and looked around him sadly. He remembered that he was alone in the big house. June had gone to Wales with Philip Bosinney to visit his relations. After yesterday's party, the house seemed quieter and more lonely than ever.

Old Jolyon thought about the events of the previous day. He had a strong love for his family and yet he had no patience[4] with some of them. He thought angrily of Soames, that 'Man of Property', who was having trouble with his wife, Irene. Now *there* was a beautiful woman, thought Old Jolyon.

The old man sighed deeply. All the members of the family had been at the party except the one he wanted to see most of all. This was his own son, Young Jolyon. Young Jolyon should have been there of course, because he was June's father. But the two Jolyons, father and son, had not met for fourteen years. To Old Jolyon, these had been fourteen wasted years.

All the trouble between father and son had begun with Young Jolyon's marriage. The old man knew now that he had been wrong in allowing his son's marriage. Was he wrong, too, in allowing June's engagement to Philip Bosinney?

Young Jolyon had been a young man when he had first got married. Old Jolyon had guessed that his son had not been in love, but he had wanted him to settle down[1]. And in four years the marriage was over. Young Jolyon had left his wife and baby daughter and had run away with a foreign girl, a governess[1]. Old Jolyon was forced to choose between his little grand-daughter, June, and his son. He had chosen to say goodbye to his son. That goodbye had lasted till now.

June's mother had died and Young Jolyon had married the foreign girl. Old Jolyon had looked after little June and had given her his love. Young Jolyon had a son now, whom Old Jolyon had never seen. They had called him Jolly, and now he had a sister, little Holly.

When Young Jolyon had married for the second time, his father had sent him a cheque for £500. Young Jolyon, who was as proud as his father, had returned the cheque. Instead, he had suggested that Old Jolyon could use the money for his grandson, little Jolly.

Old Jolyon had been very pleased with this answer. The money had been given to little Jolly and, year by year, Old Jolyon had added more money.

Young Jolyon painted pictures, and sometimes Old Jolyon had bought them to remind him of his son. But he had not hung them on his walls because they were not to his taste.

These were the thoughts of Old Jolyon as he sat alone in his study. The old man loved little children. He loved their sweetness and the way they needed help. June was grown up now and she was going to leave him. Old Jolyon longed to see his son again and his two unknown grandchildren.

Old Jolyon got slowly to his feet and lit himself a cigar.

'I'm just a lonely old man,' he said to himself. 'This house is too big for one old man. It needs a family to keep it alive.'

Old Jolyon decided to dine at his club[1] that evening. He had to do something to get out of the empty house. So he ordered his carriage, dressed carefully and drove away from Stanhope Gate.

But even in the dining-room of his club, Old Jolyon went on thinking about the past. He thought of all those times, twenty-five years ago, when his son had sat with him at the same table. How he wished that Young Jolyon was there now.

Old Jolyon had been angry with his son because Young Jolyon had caused a family scandal[1] when he had run away with that foreign governess. Old Jolyon thought about all this past unhappiness and it worried him. His son had made a mistake. Was Young Jolyon's daughter, June, going to make a mistake too? Bosinney was a strange man. June loved him more than he loved her, that was certain. All these thoughts made Old Jolyon unhappy and he did not enjoy his dinner at the club that evening. While he was drinking his coffee, he decided to go to the opera. He had not been to the opera for many years.

But even the well-loved music failed to make him happy. If only Young Jolyon had been with him! Old Jolyon felt again that he was a lonely old man. He had lost the friendship of his son. Now his grand-daughter, June, was leaving him too.

On the way home from the opera-house, an idea came to Old Jolyon. He would drive to Young Jolyon's club and ask if his son was still a member. The cab[1] drove up to the door and Old Jolyon got out.

He walked slowly up the steps and into the club. He looked round and at once a servant came up to him.

'Is Mr Jolyon Forsyte still a member here?'

'Yes, sir. He's in the club now, sir. What is your name please?'

Old Jolyon was surprised. He had not expected to speak to his son. But he answered calmly, 'Say his father would like to speak to him.'

What do a father and son say to each other when they have not met for fourteen years? Neither man wanted to show his feelings. They met and shook hands without a word. Old Jolyon could see that his son was no longer a young man. In a voice that shook a little, Old Jolyon said, 'How are you, my boy?'

The son answered, 'How are you, Dad?'

Old Jolyon's hand trembled. 'If you are going my way,' he said, 'I can take you with me.'

The two men walked down the steps together and got into the waiting cab. Old Jolyon spoke first.

'Jo,' he said. 'I should like to know about your money. I suppose you must be in debt[2].'

Old Jolyon had long ago offered his son money, but the money had been refused. Young Jolyon now had two children to look after, as well as the woman who was now his wife.

Young Jolyon answered quickly, 'No, I'm not in debt.'

Old Jolyon knew that the question had made his son angry. But he had to know the answer. The two drove on in silence until the cab reached Old Jolyon's house at Stanhope Gate.

'Come in for a moment, Jo,' Old Jolyon suggested. Now Old Jolyon had met his son, he wanted to talk to him. He was afraid of going into his great house alone.

Young Jolyon at first refused. His father knew why.

'June's not here,' said Old Jolyon quickly. 'She's away on a visit. She's engaged to be married.'

'Already?' said Young Jolyon. He still thought of his first child as a little girl. 'What is June like now?' he asked his father quietly.

'She's a little thing,' replied Old Jolyon. 'They say she looks like me, but she's more like your mother. I'll be lonely when June marries. This house is too big for an old man.'

Young Jolyon looked at his father with pity[4] as they walked into the house. The two men went into Old Jolyon's study and Young Jolyon listened quietly as the old man began to talk.

Young Jolyon looked round his father's room. It was large and dark, with heavy old furniture. Old Jolyon sat quietly in his great chair. He had lived carefully all his life. He had believed in the power of money and the importance of property. Now he owned all this property, but he was still a lonely old man.

Young Jolyon was a good listener. He listened as his father told him about his property and his money. Now and again, Young Jolyon asked a question. His eyes never left his father's face.

It was one o'clock before Old Jolyon had finished speaking. Neither of the men had talked about their own feelings. But Old Jolyon was glad he had met his son again. There was a place for Young Jolyon in his father's life now. Young Jolyon was glad, but his eyes were full of tears as he left his father's house.

Life was a difficult business, thought Young Jolyon.

The two men made no arrangements to meet again, but

Young Jolyon was a good listener.

this was not necessary. Old Jolyon needed his son now. Perhaps he also needed the love of his two little grandchildren, Jolly and Holly. Old Jolyon was a stern[4] man but he loved young children. Old Jolyon had found a new reason for living.

4

Soames Forsyte Decides to Build a House

Soames Forsyte walked out of his green front door. Looking back from across the square, Soames noticed, not for the first time, that his house needed painting.

Soames had left his wife, Irene, sitting in her room. She had been waiting for her husband to go out. She did this every day. Soames could not understand it. Why didn't Irene love him? He loved her. He gave Irene everything, but she gave him nothing. Men everywhere looked at Irene and admired her beauty, but Irene always behaved perfectly in public. It was only at home that she showed Soames her true feelings.

Soames walked quietly along the streets. He walked near the wall, quietly and carefully. He was like a cat looking out for a mouse.

Soames stopped for a moment outside a picture shop, but he saw nothing that he wanted. Soames had a fine collection of pictures; they helped to satisfy his need to own beautiful things. Irene, of course, never looked at these paintings. She never showed any interest in anything Soames did.

Before Soames moved away from the shop window, he stayed for a moment to look at his own reflection. His hair was smooth under his tall, smooth hat. His face was smooth too; his cheeks were pale and flat. It was the stern face of a man who kept his secrets.

As he walked on along the street in the same careful way as before, Soames thought again about his house, his paintings and Irene, his wife. The three problems came together in his mind. Perhaps he would leave London and move into the country. It was a good time to build a house because land was cheap. In a new house, Soames could have a special room for his paintings. Also, Irene would be away from her London friends, away from friends like June. Soames was pleased.

Then suddenly Soames had another idea. He, Soames, wanted to build a house. June's lover, Philip Bosinney, was an architect. Soames had been asking questions about Bosinney and had learnt a great deal about him.

Bosinney was a poor man, but other architects respected him. They thought his ideas were good. A poor man would not ask a high price. Soames' new house would be a bargain[2]. Soames also had the idea that Bosinney was not a good business man. If this was true, Soames would get a good house cheaply.

That evening, on his way back from the City[2] where he worked as a solicitor, Soames called at Bosinney's office. He found Bosinney at work. Soames did not waste time in polite talk.

'If you've nothing to do on Sunday,' said Soames, 'come down with me to Robin Hill. There's some land that I want you to see.'

'Are you going to build?' asked Bosinney.

'Perhaps,' said Soames, 'but don't talk about it to anyone.'

———

The following Sunday was a perfect day. Soames called for Bosinney at his rooms in the City and the two men took a train for the short journey to Robin Hill.

The countryside was beautiful, but Soames and Bosinney

looked a strange pair as they walked along the country road. Soames was correctly dressed as usual, but Bosinney wore a very odd coat with large pockets and carried a walking stick.

'Don't forget,' said Soames, looking at Bosinney carefully, 'that I want this house to be a surprise. Please don't say anything about it.

'If you tell women your plans,' Soames went on, 'you never know what will happen.' Soames didn't want Bosinney to say anything to June because she would tell Irene.

'I agree. You can't trust women. You never know what they'll do,' Bosinney replied.

Soames was surprised. He had always found women difficult to understand, but he had never said that, even to himself.

The two men reached the place that Soames had chosen for his house. But first Soames had to speak to the agent[2] who lived in a cottage nearby. Bosinney walked off by himself, while Soames talked to the agent. Soames wanted to buy land at the bottom of the hill because land was very cheap there.

After a time, Soames walked out of the cottage into the sunshine again. He smelt the freshness of the air. Soames was used to London. He felt very alone as he walked through the long grass.

Suddenly Soames caught sight of Bosinney stretched out under a large tree at the top of the hill. Soames had to touch Bosinney's arm before he looked up.

'Hello, Forsyte,' said Bosinney. 'This is the place for your house.'

Soames looked at Bosinney in surprise. 'But this land is expensive. It will cost me nearly twice as much as the land at the bottom of the hill,' Soames exclaimed angrily.

Bosinney stood up. 'Never mind the cost. Look at the view.'

The green and gold fields lay below them, stretching out to the distant hills. The sky was bright blue and the heat could almost be seen. As Soames looked, the beauty became part of

Soames caught sight of Bosinney stretched out
under a large tree.

him. He wanted to own all this beauty just as, four years before, he had wanted to own Irene.

'I could build you a fine house here,' said Bosinney, 'for eight thousand pounds. It would be like a palace.'

'I can't afford it,' said Soames. But Soames knew that he could afford it and that he would find the money.

Before the two men left Robin Hill, Soames spoke to the agent and agreed to buy the land at the top of the hill. It would be a fine place for Irene. Surely she would be happy there.

As he had planned, Soames said nothing to Irene about the house. As Bosinney had said, women cannot be trusted.

Exactly a week later, Soames and Irene were having dinner alone in their small, elegant¹ dining-room. The food was very good and the dining-table looked beautiful. Irene, beautifully dressed as usual, sat in the pink glow of a soft light. They looked a perfect couple, but all through the meal they had not spoken one word to each other.

There was a strange look on Irene's face and Soames was worried. At last he said, 'Has anyone been here this afternoon?'

'June,' replied Irene.

'Now what did she want?' asked Soames, not pleased. 'I suppose she came to talk about Bosinney. I think that she loves him more than he loves her.'

'Please don't say that,' said Irene quickly. 'It's not true.'

'Of course, I know you are June's friend,' said Soames with a smile. 'But she'll soon be too busy to worry about you. In any case, you won't see so much of her soon. We're going to live in the country.'

Soames expected Irene to be surprised or even angry, but she said nothing.

'You don't seem interested,' said Soames, looking at his wife carefully.

'I know about it already,' Irene replied quickly.

'Who told you?' asked Soames.

'June.'

Irene's short answers made Soames uncomfortable.

'It will be a good thing for Bosinney,' he said. 'It's an important job for him.'

Irene said nothing, so Soames went on. 'I suppose you don't want to live in the country. But you never seem happy here.'

Irene stood up gracefully and looked at her husband.

'Does it matter what I want?' she said. 'Does it matter if I am unhappy?'

She went out of the room and left Soames seated at the table.

At first he was angry. Was he going to spend nearly ten thousand pounds for a woman like this? Then he became calmer. Bosinney would build him a beautiful house and would charge him less than any other architect. Soames would get a bargain and would have a beautiful piece of property to hold his paintings and his wife. Soames decided to be content.

5

The Plans of the House

Soames wanted to keep the new house a secret from his family, but of course, he could not. Very soon, all the Forsytes were talking about Soames' plan to build a new house in the country.

The Forsytes all lived in London now, but the father of Old Jolyon, James and Swithin had lived in the country for most of his life. He had been a farmer in Dorset and then, later, a builder. At the end of his life, the old man had moved to London and built houses there. He had died a very rich man. Now Soames, James' son, was going to live in the country.

The Forsytes found this very interesting.

James was worried about Soames' plan to build a house. He thought that his son was making a mistake and would have to spend far too much money. After thinking about the new house for some time, James decided to visit Soames and Irene. He wanted to give his son some advice and find out about the house, too.

Irene invited James to dinner and talked charmingly to the old man. James ate the good food with enjoyment and drank a little wine. His daughter-in-law was really a very beautiful woman and she managed the house well. Looking at Irene, James stopped worrying about Soames and his money.

After dinner, Soames went to look at his paintings. James was left alone with Irene who sat quietly in her chair. What was Irene thinking about? James could not tell. He decided to ask her a few questions.

'What do you do all day?' James asked. 'I suppose June comes here a lot. What about that young Bosinney? Now what do you think of him?'

'Mr Bosinney is planning a house for Soames,' said Irene, not answering James' questions.

'My advice,' said James, 'is don't have too much to do with Bosinney.'

Irene's only answer was a smile – a smile of great power and beauty. James looked at her sharply.

'I don't think you have enough to do. You ought to have a child,' he said.

Irene said nothing, but the smile left her face and her whole body became hard and completely still.

'Well, I don't know,' said James. 'Nobody tells me anything. You and Soames must know your own business.'

Irene did not answer him and soon afterwards James went home. He had found out nothing at all.

So the plans for the house went on. Bosinney was very

busy. He had no time to visit June now and no time to go out with her.

After weeks of hard work, the plans were finished and Bosinney took them to Soames' house where he met Irene.

Soames was glad to see that Irene liked Bosinney. She seemed happy when she was talking to him.

Bosinney spread out the plans on a large table and Soames looked at them carefully. He was surprised because they were not what he had expected.

'It's a strange kind of house,' Soames said at last. 'There seems to be a lot of wasted space.'

Bosinney began to walk up and down the room like an angry animal.

'This is a house for a gentleman,' he said. 'You will have space to live here. Look, this long room is for your paintings.'

Soames was interested and looked at the plans again.

'The rooms are very big,' he said. 'They may be cold. Irene feels the cold.'

'Irene won't be cold,' Bosinney answered. 'I have planned to have hot-water heating.'

Soames was still not happy. 'Won't this house cost me a lot of money?' he asked.

Bosinney took a piece of paper from his pocket. 'If the materials are good – and they must be good – the house will cost you £8500.'

Soames was both surprised and angry at this answer. 'But that's £500 more than the amount I agreed to,' he said.

'I can't do it for a penny less,' said Bosinney. He spoke clearly and sharply. Soames looked surprised, but said nothing. Bosinney had spoken to him in the right way.

Soames was really very pleased with the plans and could see that Bosinney was a clever architect. This house would be a beautiful and unusual piece of property. So Soames agreed to the plans and even invited Bosinney to stay for lunch.

During lunch, Bosinney and Irene talked together happily. They hardly noticed when Soames left the room and went upstairs to look at his paintings.

When he came back, Soames was pleased to see that Irene and Bosinney were still talking together like old friends. He thought that Irene was looking even more beautiful than usual.

When Bosinney had gone home, Soames said, 'Well, Irene, what do you think of "The Buccaneer"?'

Irene looked at the floor and Soames waited for her answer.

'I don't know,' Irene said at last.

'Do you think he's good-looking?' Soames asked his wife.

Irene smiled in a strange way that Soames could not understand.

'Yes, very,' she said.

6

Soames and Bosinney Disagree

And so the new house was started. The weather was good and the work went on slowly all through the winter and the spring.

By the end of April, the walls were finished and the roof was on. Soames went down to Robin Hill many times and walked quietly about the building, studying everything with the greatest care. He often made the workmen angry by asking them questions about their work.

On the last day of April, Soames arranged to meet Bosinney at Robin Hill. He wanted to talk to him about the money he was spending. The bills[2] had been worrying Soames and he looked at all of them carefully, adding them up several times. At last he spoke to Bosinney.

'I can't understand,' Soames said, 'why you have spent so

much money. These bills add up to £700 more than the amount we agreed to. This is too much. I'm sure you can do the work more cheaply than this.'

Bosinney was angry, but he spoke quietly. 'No, I can't,' he said. 'I've saved every penny I can.'

'But this is far more than I want to pay,' Soames replied.

'I wish I had never agreed to plan your house,' said Bosinney, standing up quickly. 'You are always coming here with your own ideas. You make the workmen angry with your questions and you make me angry too. If you don't like my work, I'll leave at once. But if you have another architect, you'll have to pay him much more than you're paying me.'

Bosinney looked so angry and so like a 'buccaneer' that Soames was a little frightened. Soames liked the house because it was interesting and unusual, and he wanted it finished quickly so that he and Irene could live there.

'All right,' said Soames, 'but please be very careful. And I want to have another look at everything you have done.'

While the two men walked slowly round the unfinished house, Bosinney told Soames his ideas.

'I want the colours to be exactly right,' Bosinney said. 'I want Irene to hear my ideas. She understands beauty and she will understand what I want.'

'I suppose you think that Irene is beautiful too,' said Soames.

'Yes,' said Bosinney sharply and he walked away quickly.

Soames loved beautiful things, but he could not understand a man like Philip Bosinney. Bosinney was an artist and beauty was more important to him than property. He was building the house for Irene, not for Soames.

7

An Evening at the Theatre

That same evening, Bosinney and June were having dinner
with Irene and Soames. Afterwards, Bosinney was taking
June to the theatre. They had not been out together for a long
time and June was looking forward to the evening very much.
Bosinney was often too busy to take her out now because the
house took all his time. June was sure that they would enjoy
themselves. She was going to show Bosinney just how much she
loved him.

June dressed with great care and arrived at Soames' house
early. She was wearing a very pretty white dress which made her
red-gold hair look very beautiful.

The servant told June that Bosinney was already in the
house. June wanted to give him a surprise, so she opened the
drawing-room door quietly. The long room was full of the scent
of flowers. June could hear Bosinney's voice, but she could not
see him.

'I have so much to say to you,' Bosinney was saying, 'but
now we won't have time.'

Irene's voice answered. 'We can talk at dinner.'

'But I won't be able to talk to you at dinner,' Bosinney
continued. 'Come down to the house on Sunday. We can be
alone there.'

Irene looked up and saw June standing by the door. The two
women looked at each other. Bosinney was standing with his
back to the door and had not realized that June was in the
room.

'I've promised to go for a drive with Uncle Swithin on
Sunday,' said Irene. She still spoke to Bosinney as though June
was not in the room.

Irene looked up and and saw June standing by the door.

'Make him bring you to Robin Hill,' said Bosinney softly. 'Please do. I must see you there. I thought that you wanted to help me.'

Irene answered so softly that her voice seemed like the movement of the flowers.

'So I do. I do want to help you.'

June could listen no longer and moved forward quickly.

'How hot it is in here,' she said clearly. 'I hate the smell of these flowers. They give me a headache.'

June looked at Irene and Bosinney angrily. 'Were you talking about the house?' she asked them. 'I haven't seen it yet. Why don't we all go down there on Sunday?'

'I can't go. I'm going for a drive with Uncle Swithin,' replied Irene.

There was an uncomfortable silence. June heard a movement behind her and turned round. Soames had come into the room.

'Well,' said Irene, looking at them all. 'If we are all ready, dinner is ready too.'

The four young people moved silently into the dining-room and sat down at the table. June ate and drank very little. She was too unhappy. Most of the time, Irene talked to Bosinney. Behind Soames, the sunset filled the room with warm, golden light.

'If only ...,' said Irene softly.

'Only what?' said June.

'If only it could always be spring,' continued Irene.

June said nothing.

At last it was time for June and Bosinney to go out to the theatre. Irene, standing near the window said, 'Such a lovely night.'

And Soames added, 'I hope you both enjoy yourselves.'

June made Bosinney take her on the top of a bus. The bus had no roof and June wanted to breathe the fresh air. She could still smell the heavy scent of the flowers in Irene's room and her head ached.

Spring had come to London and the trees in Hyde Park were covered with leaves and flowers. Men and women walked slowly through the streets, enjoying the beauty of the spring evening.

It was a time to be happy. But June and Bosinney did not have anything to say to each other. They went into the theatre in silence. In silence, they walked slowly up the stairs and got to their seats just before the play began.

June knew very well that Philip Bosinney's feelings for her had changed. Now she knew why. He found her friend Irene more beautiful and more interesting than June herself. She sat very still, but her mind was full of jealous thoughts and questions.

The first part of the play came to an end. June had not heard a word.

'It's hot in here,' June said. 'I want to go out.' Her face was very white.

'I want to say something to you, Phil,' she said, when they had left their seats.

'Yes?' said Bosinney. His hard voice struck June like cold water.

June spoke quickly. 'You don't let me be nice to you, Phil. You know I want to do everything for you.'

June stopped for a moment and then said, 'Phil, take me to see the house on Sunday.'

Bosinney looked worried. 'Not Sunday, dear. Some other day,' he replied.

'Why not Sunday? I wouldn't get in your way.'

'I have an engagement[1],' said Bosinney.

'You are going to take — ' June began. But Bosinney's eyes flashed with anger and June was afraid to finish her sentence.

The two walked back slowly to their seats. Hot tears were

running down June's pale face and she could see nothing.

After the play was over, Bosinney took June back to her grandfather's house. Bosinney said goodbye to her quickly. He seemed to be thinking about something else and did not say when he would see June again. When she was alone, June walked slowly into the big, old house. She wanted to go straight up to her own room, but Old Jolyon heard her and called her into his study.

'You're very late,' he said kindly. 'Where have you been?'

'We had dinner at Soames',' June replied.

'Oh yes,' said Old Jolyon, 'the Man of Property. His wife was there of course, and Bosinney too, I suppose?'

'Yes.'

Old Jolyon looked at June with his sharp old eyes. He kissed his grand-daughter and said, 'Goodnight, my darling,' in a voice that shook a little.

'I knew she would have trouble with that Bosinney,' said Old Jolyon to himself after June had left the room. 'He goes to Soames' house too often. Bosinney isn't a bad man; he works hard and he isn't interested in June's money. But he doesn't seem interested in June either. But June is a Forsyte. She is stubborn, like her father and like me. She still wants to marry Bosinney, but he doesn't want her now. What will happen to my little June?'

Old Jolyon sighed heavily. His son, Young Jolyon, had been unhappy for many years and now his grand-daughter, June, was unhappy too. Love caused this unhappiness. What a trouble it was. For the first time, Old Jolyon felt that he really was an old man.

Upstairs, June sat in her room by the open window. She could not sleep. She breathed in the heavy scents of the spring night and cried for her lost lover and her own unhappiness.

8

A Drive with Uncle Swithin

The following Sunday, Uncle Swithin, Old Jolyon's brother, dressed himself with the greatest care. He was going to drive Irene to Robin Hill.

When he was younger, Swithin had been famous for his horses and for his smart carriage. He was an old man now, but he still enjoyed a drive. Most of all, he enjoyed driving with a pretty woman, but he hadn't done that for years. Now he was talking Irene down to Robin Hill and this made the old man very proud and happy.

The weather was beautiful and Swithin's horses looked fine. He thought that they were the best in London. Swithin looked at them carefully and then made sure that there was a rug in the open carriage. The day was as warm as summer, but Swithin did not want Irene to catch cold.

Slowly, Swithin moved his old body onto the high driving-seat and took the reins in his old hands. He sat straight and looked around him proudly. Then he shook the reins and the horses moved forward.

When Swithin reached Soames' house, Irene was waiting for him and came out of the house straight away. As usual, she was beautifully dressed and her dark eyes shone softly. Swithin was very happy to see her. He enjoyed talking to Irene. Also, he wanted to see the house at Robin Hill for himself.

The sun was hot and the long drive made Swithin feel sleepy. He had not driven so far for a long time and he almost fell asleep while he was driving.

Bosinney was waiting at Robin Hill when Swithin and Irene drove up, and the three of them went into the house together.

Swithin moved slowly round the house, leaning heavily on his stick. He did not really understand the plan of the house, but he liked some parts of the building.

'That's a fine staircase,' said Swithin, pointing at it with his stick. 'But you need some statues there.'

Irene looked at Swithin with her soft, bright eyes. Swithin noticed that Irene was listening carefully. She would take his advice, he knew.

Swithin said little about the rooms, but he was very pleased with the cellar.

'You'll be able to store hundreds of bottles of wine here,' he said. 'Very fine, indeed.'

'Why don't you look at the house from outside?' Bosinney suggested to Swithin. He had noticed that the old man was beginning to move more slowly. They went outside.

'There's a fine view from here,' said Swithin, 'but have you a chair? I would like to sit down.'

Bosinney brought out a chair from the house and Swithin slowly lowered his heavy body on to it. There he sat in the hot sun while Bosinney and Irene walked slowly down the hill. They stopped once or twice to wave to Swithin. At first, he waved back. Then slowly his head fell on to his chest and he was asleep.

No one saw Bosinney and Irene walking under the trees. No one saw them stop, turn and look at each other. No one heard Bosinney cry out, 'You must know. I love you.' No one saw them kiss under the moving light of the trees.

Swithin woke up suddenly. Where were those two young people? He stood up and looked around him. There they were, with Irene walking in front. 'The Buccaneer', young Bosinney, was following behind holding a handkerchief tightly in his hand. As they came nearer, Swithin felt that there was something strange about young Bosinney. What was it?

Then suddenly an idea came to Swithin. 'I think he's in

No one saw Bosinney and Irene walking under the trees.

love with Mrs Soames,' Swithin thought to himself. But although Swithin looked sharply at Irene and Philip Bosinney, he said nothing.

Irene walked slowly back to Swithin's open carriage. Swithin noticed that Bosinney held Irene's hand for several seconds as they said goodbye.

On the way home, Swithin talked a good deal and told Irene all his worries about his house and his servants. Irene said nothing, but Swithin was sure that she was listening carefully.

Swithin had driven for some miles, when he realized that someone was following his carriage and coming nearer and nearer. It was a young man in a donkey-cart and he was driving much too fast. He was trying to go faster than Swithin and this made the old man very angry. He refused to be passed by a poor young man in a donkey-cart.

Suddenly, the wheels of the cart touched the wheels of Swithin's carriage. The donkey-cart turned over and the young man was thrown out on to the road.

Swithin did not turn round or stop the carriage. He could not. His horses were badly frightened. They were going very fast now and the carriage swung from side to side. Swithin had to hold on to the reins with all his strength.

'Are we going to have an accident, Uncle Swithin?' said Irene in her quiet voice, as she held tightly to the side of the carriage.

'Don't move,' cried Swithin. 'Don't worry. I'll get you home.'

'I don't care if I never get home,' said Irene. It was a terrible moment for Swithin and he could not believe what he had heard.

At last the frightened horses slowed down. The danger was over.

After Swithin had left Irene at the door of her own house, he drove straight to his sisters' house. He had to tell them

Swithin did not turn round or stop.

what Irene had said. 'I don't care if I never get home.' No wife should say that.

Irene had a beautiful home and her husband gave her everything she wanted. But instead of loving her husband, Irene was in love with another man – a poor man without property. Swithin and his sisters were very worried. They could not understand Irene at all. She would make poor, dear Soames very unhappy and the family did not want another scandal.

9

'A Free Hand'

Soon everyone in the family knew what Irene had said. There were other things to talk about too. Someone had seen dear June at the theatre with Philip Bosinney. June had looked very unhappy and the two had left the theatre early. Irene and Bosinney had been seen together several times in shops or in the park.

All the Forsytes thought about Young Jolyon although they had not spoken about him for many years. They remembered how Old Jolyon's son had fallen in love with another woman and caused a scandal. These things could happen, even in the Forsyte family.

Soames' father, James, was extremely worried about all this talk. He was too old to remember the feelings of a man in love. The thought of what might happen filled him with fear.

The house at Robin Hill had made all this trouble, James decided. Why had Soames wanted a house in the country? Why had he chosen young Bosinney to be the architect? And now Soames was spending far too much money, James was sure.

James was so worried that he went down to Robin Hill to see the house for himself.

Bosinney was angry when James came to the house. He showed James everything, but he spoke rudely to the old man. When James was going to leave, Bosinney questioned him sharply.

'Are any more of you coming down here? If they are, I should like to know about it.'

James did not know what to say. After a few moments, he left Bosinney and walked slowly back to the station to catch the train to London.

The next day, James went to see Soames at his office. James said nothing to his son about his visit to the house.

Soames was sitting at his desk with a letter in his hand.

'I think you should see this,' Soames said and he gave the letter to his father. The letter was from Philip Bosinney.

---

309 Sloane Street
May 15th

Dear Forsyte,

Your house is finished and my work there is finished too. If you want me to decorate the house, I must have a free hand[2].

You keep coming down to Robin Hill and telling me what to do. You worry me by writing letters. Yesterday your father came to see the house too.

I would rather not work for you any more, but if I do, I must be left alone to do things in my own way. I must have a free hand.

Yours truly,

Philip Bosinney

'What are you going to say to him?' asked James.

'I haven't made up my mind,' said Soames, not looking at his father.

But Soames had made a plan. He had decided to show the letter to his uncle, Old Jolyon. Why did he want to do this? Soames was not really sure himself. But Old Jolyon was the head of the family and everyone knew that he could think clearly and give good advice.

So the next day, Soames took Bosinney's letter to Old Jolyon.

'I've had this letter from Bosinney,' Soames told him. 'I thought you should know. I've already spent far too much money on the house.'

'It's clear enough,' said Old Jolyon, when he had read the letter.

'I don't know what a "free hand" means,' said Soames. 'It may mean that I will have to spend a lot more money.'

'If you don't trust Bosinney, why do you ask him to work for you?' asked Old Jolyon.

'Perhaps you could speak to him, Uncle Jolyon,' said Soames. 'You are the head of the family. And you are well-known as a business man. He would listen carefully to you.'

'No,' said Old Jolyon. 'I'll have nothing to do with it.'

'Well,' said Soames. 'You are June's grandfather. You should know my feelings. I don't want any trouble.'

Soames was talking about his wife and her feelings for Bosinney, as Old Jolyon knew very well.

'I don't want to know about your problems,' said Old Jolyon sharply.

'Very well,' said Soames. 'I just thought I should tell you. Good morning.' And the two men parted, both feeling angry.

In the afternoon, Soames answered Bosinney's letter. He thought carefully about every word.

> 62 Montpelier Square
> May 17th 1887
>
> Dear Bosinney,
>
> Your letter surprised me. All your plans have been
> completed and no one has changed them. I will give you a
> 'free hand', but you must understand one thing. The total
> cost of the house – the land, the building and the decora-
> tions – must not be more than £12 000. This is much
> more than I wanted to pay. It will be more than enough.
> I am,
> Yours truly,
>
> Soames Forsyte

Bosinney's answer was short.

> 309 Sloane Street
> May 18th
>
> Dear Forsyte,
>
> I am an artist, not a businessman. I cannot promise to
> spend no more than £12 000. I cannot work for you any
> more.
> Yours faithfully,
>
> Philip Bosinney

Soames thought for a long time before writing an answer to
this letter. He wanted Bosinney to do the work because he
knew that Bosinney would do it well. But Soames was afraid of
spending too much money. At last Soames behaved like a 'Man
of Property'. He could not lose the house now.

It was beautiful and he must have it. More than anything

else, he wanted to live there with Irene. He wrote:

> *May 19th 1887*
>
> *Dear Bosinney,*
>
> *I want you to finish your work for me. You can spend a little more than £12 000 if you find it necessary. You can spend up to £50 more than this if you have to. That is what I meant by a 'free hand'.*
>
> *Soames Forsyte*

Bosinney's answer contained only two words.

> *May 20th*
>
> *Dear Forsyte,*
> *Very well.*
>
> *P. Bosinney*

10

Old Jolyon at the Zoo

Old Jolyon had been unhappy for some time. His talk with Soames about the house had made him angry. In Old Jolyon's opinion, Soames was a hard man with no feelings[4].

In some ways, Old Jolyon was sorry for Irene, but he worried most of all about June. She was thin and pale and Old Jolyon was sure that she cried a lot. Worst of all, she told Old Jolyon nothing about her troubles. It was all the fault of that Bosinney, Old Jolyon thought. Bosinney was not being kind or fair to June.

Old Jolyon needed the company of young people and he began to see more of Young Jolyon and his children. Little Holly and Jolly, Old Jolyon's grandchildren, were a very great pleasure to the old man and Young Jolyon loved to see them together.

Today they were all at the zoo, a place the children loved. Old Jolyon walked slowly along in the sunshine, Holly on one side of him and Jolly on the other. Young Jolyon walked beside them, a smile on his pleasant face, although he did not care very much for the zoo. The animals in the cages reminded him that many people like himself were not really free. But he liked to see his father looking happy.

As they were leaving the zoo, Old Jolyon at last spoke to his son about June.

'I don't know what to do,' Old Jolyon said. 'June is so unhappy, but she won't tell me anything. That Bosinney is behaving badly. I should like to hit him.'

'What has he done?' asked Young Jolyon quietly. 'It's better that June doesn't marry him if he doesn't love her.'

'I suppose you think that he has done nothing wrong,' said Old Jolyon. He could not keep the anger out of his voice. He remembered that his own son had behaved in the same way as Bosinney, fourteen years before.

Young Jolyon knew what his father was thinking. 'I suppose Bosinney has fallen in love with another woman,' he said at last.

'So the family says,' replied his father. 'They say he's in love with Soames' wife.'

Young Jolyon knew that Irene had been June's friend. 'Poor little June,' he said. He saw that his own unhappy story was being repeated. His daughter, June, was being made unhappy and Young Jolyon could not help her.

Old Jolyon was sorry now that he had told his son about Bosinney.

*Old Jolyon walked slowly along, Holly on one side of him
and Jolly on the other.*

'I don't believe a word of it,' the old man added as he said goodbye to his son and grandchildren. 'There's too much talk, as usual.'

But Old Jolyon did not really believe his own words. He had heard the family talking together and he knew all these stories were true. He had tried to stop his brothers and sisters talking about Bosinney and Soames' wife, but he knew that he could not.

11

The Dance

Now the Forsytes began to watch Irene and Bosinney very carefully when they saw them together. June was not often seen at parties now. She felt too tired and unhappy. Old Jolyon was worried to see his grand-daughter so pale and ill. Usually, June was full of life and energy, but now she moved slowly and took no interest in anything.

Then, one morning at breakfast, June told her grandfather about a dance that was going to be held at one of the Forsytes' houses.

'I want to go,' June said. 'But I suppose it's too late now. I have no one to go with.'

In the past, June and Irene had gone to dances together.

Old Jolyon looked at June keenly. 'Why don't you ask Irene?' he said.

'Oh no, grandfather. I don't want to ask Irene. But you could take me, grandfather. Please do. Just for a short time.'

And June looked at Old Jolyon with such a happy look in her eyes that the old man agreed.

On the day of the dance, June seemed happy and excited.

But after lunch, she went up to her room and cried all the afternoon. When Old Jolyon saw her at dinner, he said that they would not go out. June must go to bed.

But at ten o'clock, June spoke to her maid. 'Please tell Mr Forsyte I am perfectly well. If he cannot go, I shall go to the dance by myself,' she said.

June had decided that Philip Bosinney would love her again, when he saw her looking happy at the dance.

She dressed herself with great care and she left she house with Old Jolyon at about eleven o'clock.

Soames saw them arrive. Because he did not like to dance, he was standing by himself at a lighted window. Soames was surprised to see Old Jolyon arrive so late.

Soames looked at June with his careful smile. He had not seen her for some time. He noticed how pale and tired she seemed. Suddenly, Soames saw June's face become even paler.

Soames turned to see what June was looking at. He saw his wife, Irene, coming into the room with Philip Bosinney. They were talking quietly and they were looking into each others' eyes. Soames looked again at June. She was saying something to Old Jolyon. Old Jolyon looked at her in surprise and then, without speaking, he and June turned and walked quickly from the house.

Irene and Bosinney passed close to where Soames was standing and Soames could smell the flowers on Irene's dress. There was a look on her face that he had never seen before.

Irene held Bosinney tightly as they danced and her dark eyes gazed at his face.

Very white, Soames turned and looked out of the window. He was just in time to see June and Old Jolyon get into their carriage and drive away.

On the way home, June cried so much that her whole body shook. Old Jolyon tried to stop her crying, but he could not.

Other people had seen Irene Forsyte and Bosinney dancing

There was a look on Irene's face that Soames had never seen before.

together. Other people had seen June and her grandfather leave the dance after only a few minutes. All the Forsytes were talking about the scandal now.

Then came the news that Old Jolyon had taken June to the sea for a holiday. The Forsytes waited. What would Bosinney and Irene do next? Irene was bored of course, said the young Forsytes. Soames was very dull. Why shouldn't she amuse herself?

It was a beautiful summer. The park was full of the scent of flowers. The sun shone all day and at night people had their meals in the open air.

At the end of June, Soames' sister, Winifred, decided to find out what was happening for herself.

Dear Irene, (she wrote)
    I hear that Soames will be away tomorrow night. Let's go to Richmond for dinner. The river looks lovely now. Will you ask Mr Bosinney to come and I will bring another man.
    Your affectionate sister-in-law,

Winifred.   *Winifred*

Winifred did not want to take her own husband to Richmond. He often drank too much. Also Winifred knew that her husband thought Irene was very beautiful. He would want to talk to Irene all the evening and he would probably try to kiss her too. But Winifred could not find another man to go with her, so she had to ask her husband, Dartie, after all.

Winifred and Dartie drove to Richmond together. Irene and Bosinney drove in another carriage and were already in the hotel when Winifred and her husband arrived.

Dartie ordered a good meal and a good deal of wine too. Dartie tried hard to make Irene talk to him, but she said very little. Dartie looked hard at Bosinney from time to time, but he could not understand what the young man was thinking.

At the end of the meal, all of them went for a walk by the river. The air was warm and full of the sounds of voices – the voices of happy people, enjoying themselves.

After a time, they all sat down on a long seat near the river.

Dartie made sure that he sat next to Irene. He had drunk a lot of wine and he sat as close to Irene as he could. What a beautiful woman she was! But Irene said nothing to Dartie when he spoke to her. Bosinney sat on the other side of Dartie. There was a look of great pain on his face. Dartie could see this and it made him smile. Irene and Bosinney were in love, that was certain.

When the time came to go home, Dartie walked close to Irene. Dartie had a plan. He had decided he would go home in the same carriage as Irene. Then Bosinney would have to go back with Winifred.

Winifred got into her carriage first. Dartie stood waiting by the door of the other carriage for Irene. But Bosinney suddenly came close to him in the darkness and spoke in a quiet, angry voice.

'I am taking Irene back. Do you understand?'

'What? No. You go back with my wife,' replied Dartie.

'Get away,' said Bosinney, 'or I will knock you over.' And before Dartie could reply, Bosinney had helped Irene into the empty carriage and it had driven off very fast.

Dartie could do nothing.

'Why didn't you stop them?' he shouted to his wife. 'Can't you see Bosinney is in love with your brother's wife?'

Winifred said nothing.

In the other carriage, Bosinney told Irene of his love. Irene held his hand and cried softly in the darkness. She loved Bosinney, but already she understood that Soames would never let her go.

When the carriage reached Soames' house, Irene got out quickly and was soon inside the house.

Dartie and his wife went home too. They decided not to say anything about what had happened.

Long after the other three were asleep, Bosinney walked in the darkness through the empty streets. He returned to the house where Irene lived and, for a long time, looked up at the dark windows. Irene was now more important to Philip Bosinney than his own life.

12

'I Can Hold On Too'

Young Jolyon Forsyte knew that he was different from the rest of his family in several ways. He had left his wife for another woman and caused a family scandal. He had lived his own life away from the rest of the Forsytes for many years. Because of this, he was able to watch the other members of the family as though he was a stranger.

After his wife died, Young Jolyon married the woman he had run away with. Everyone thought that he had behaved foolishly and, in a way, he knew this to be true. But he had lived his life in his own way and had found some happiness. He was able to understand what people felt when they fell in love. He would never blame anyone who did this.

When Young Jolyon received a letter from his father about June, he understood for the first time how worried Old Jolyon was.

'June is not at all well,' Old Jolyon wrote. 'Our holiday by the sea is not doing her any good. She is far too unhappy.

Someone ought to speak to Bosinney. Someone must ask him if he is going to marry June or not. Perhaps you could do this. Perhaps you could speak to Bosinney. We must know the truth for June's sake.'

Young Jolyon thought for a long time about the letter his father had written. Of course, he wanted to help June. But Young Jolyon believed that people should do what they wanted to do. If Bosinney loved Irene, he must not marry June.

While Young Jolyon was still thinking about the letter, he met Bosinney by chance. He noticed that Bosinney had become thinner and that he looked very unhappy. Young Jolyon spoke first.

'I haven't seen you for a long time,' he said. 'How are you getting on with Soames' house?'

'It will be finished in about a week,' Bosinney replied.

'That's good. It must have been a difficult job,' said Young Jolyon. 'You must be glad that the work is nearly over. But I suppose you feel sorry too. That's the way I feel when I finish painting a picture.'

Bosinney was interested in what Young Jolyon had said. 'I didn't know you painted,' he answered.

'Oh yes,' said young Jolyon. 'And that makes me different from most other Forsytes. But I am a Forsyte, you know. And a Forsyte likes his property. A Forsyte doesn't give up anything easily – a house, a picture or even a woman. We Forsytes are all like that.'

The two men looked at each other. Bosinney knew what Young Jolyon was telling him. He was telling him that Soames would never give up Irene. He would never let her go.

'Of course,' Young Jolyon said, 'I behaved differently, many years ago. But, because I am a Forsyte, I held on to what I wanted. I married the woman that I loved.'

'Thank you,' said Bosinney, with a strange smile, 'but I am like you. I know what I want and I can hold on to it, too.'

Bosinney walked quickly away and Young Jolyon looked after him sadly. He could understand Bosinney's feelings about Irene, but he could also understand Soames' feelings. Soames was a Forsyte. He would hold on to his property even if it made him very unhappy.

'Soames will never give up Irene because she is his wife,' thought Young Jolyon. 'And Bosinney won't give her up either.'

Young Jolyon could see great unhappiness for all of them. But he could do nothing to help.

13

'Will You Let Me Go?'

The next day, Soames did not have much work to do in his office. He left early and walked home as usual, where he found Irene sitting quietly in the drawing-room. This was strange because she went out nearly every afternoon now.

'Why are you at home?' Soames asked his wife. 'Are you waiting for anyone?'

'Mr Bosinney said he might come.'

'Bosinney,' said Soames. 'He ought to be working. I want you to come out with me into the park, as we used to. We could sit under the trees.'

'I don't want to go out,' said Irene. 'I have a headache.'

'You always have a headache when I ask you to do something,' Soames answered sharply.

'I try to do what you want me to,' Irene said quietly, 'but I can't. Before we married you promised me something. You promised to let me go if our marriage was not a success.'

Soames was surprised and angry at Irene's words.

'It would be a success if you behaved properly,' he told his wife.

'I have tried,' Irene replied. 'Will you let me go?'

'Let you go? What are you talking about?' asked Soames. He did not know what to say to Irene.

'I won't hear such nonsense,' Soames went on. 'We will go out – or are you waiting for Bosinney to come?'

Without a word, Irene stood up.

The two unhappy people walked slowly out of the house, along the busy streets into Hyde Park. Soames led Irene to a place in the park where many fashionable people were walking. He made his wife sit next to him on a long seat under the trees. Irene was still his property. He wanted everyone to see them together.

As Soames and Irene sat in silence, Bosinney walked past. He had just been to Soames' house and of course had found no one at home.

Soames stood up as Bosinney stopped in front of him.

'We're just going back,' Soames said. 'Come back with us for dinner.'

Soames invited Bosinney because he knew that Bosinney could not refuse. Soames did not really want to see Bosinney in his house. He just wanted to show the young man that Irene had a good home and belonged only to her husband.

Soames talked to Bosinney in a friendly way all through dinner. He refused to look at Irene and Bosinney when they said goodbye, later on. He knew for sure now that Bosinney loved his wife. Soames was unhappy – as unhappy as Bosinney and Irene. But Young Jolyon had been right. Soames would never give up his property, however unhappy it made him.

———

Soames got up next day, still full of anger. He hated Bosinney with all his heart. Soames thought of the house at Robin Hill. It was finished now and Soames, in his strange way, was very pleased with it. Pleased, until he looked again at the bills and saw the amount of money Bosinney had spent. To his surprise, Soames saw that Bosinney had spent more money than the amount he had agreed to.

Bosinney had wanted the house to be perfect for Irene because he loved her. He did not understand Soames' feelings about money. Had Bosinney forgotten Soames' letter to him? It was more likely that he just did not care. To Bosinney, the perfection of the house was much more important than a few hundred pounds.

Soames' anger with Irene made him more angry with Bosinney.

'Your friend the Buccaneer will pay for this,' said Soames to Irene at breakfast. 'He's made a fool of himself this time.'

'I don't know what you are talking about,' said Irene coldly.

'Well then, I will tell you,' Soames replied. 'He has spent £350 more than we agreed. So he can pay that money himself. I won't.'

'But you know that Bosinney has no money,' cried Irene.

'He must find the money somehow,' Soames replied.

'Then you are meaner[4] than I thought you were,' Irene told her husband.

Her answer made Soames so angry that he asked Irene a direct question.

'Are you in love with Bosinney?'

Irene gave no answer.

'I believe you are made of stone[4],' said Soames looking at her face. 'Some husbands would beat you. That would make you speak the truth.'

Soames knew that he had said too much. During the day, he decided that he would apologize to Irene. But it was too late. When he went up to their room that night, Soames found that

Irene had locked their bedroom door. He called out to her to open it. Irene was moving about the room softly, but she did not answer.

'She must really hate me,' thought Soames. He had not believed it before, but now he knew. The only time that Irene was happy was when she was out of the house, away from her husband.

———

All through the summer and autumn, the house at Robin Hill stood empty. Irene refused to leave London. Soames was certain that she met Bosinney nearly every day, but he could not stop her. The Buccaneer never came to Soames' house now so Soames never saw him, but Soames thought about Bosinney all the time. In his mind he could see the meetings between Philip Bosinney and Irene.

One day, Young Jolyon saw Irene and Bosinney together in the park. Young Jolyon, who was painting, was hidden behind some trees. He stood very still and watched Irene and Bosinney as they walked slowly over the grass. He looked at them with great pity.

Young Jolyon remembered the time fourteen years ago when he had met a young woman in secret. He remembered how he had been both happy and unhappy in the same way as Irene and Bosinney were now.

'What will Soames do?' Young Jolyon thought. 'He will not allow this to go on. He will do something to hurt Irene by ruining[2] Bosinney. And what about June? Bosinney will never marry her now.'

Young Jolyon thought about his father too. He knew how unhappy the old man was about his grand-daughter. Old Jolyon needed his son more and more now. He often visited Young Jolyon's little house, talking to him and playing with little

Jolly and Holly. Old Jolyon's sharp old eyes had noticed how poor his son's house was. He made up his mind to help his son immediately.

Old Jolyon had given his son a good deal of money. He had also changed his will[3] to make sure that Young Jolyon would be a very rich man after his death. Young Jolyon would become a 'man of property' himself. Old Jolyon was very pleased when he thought that Young Jolyon would one day have more money than Soames.

If money alone can make a man happy, Young Jolyon's story would have a happy ending. But things were going to be very different for Irene and Philip Bosinney. They had no money, no way of escape.

14

Bosinney in the Fog

Soames had made a decision. He had decided to take Bosinney to court. The architect had spent too much of Soames' money on the house at Robin Hill. If Soames won the case[3], he would get the extra money back and Bosinney would be ruined.

Soames was an extremely careful man. As a solicitor, he had been trained to read men's words very carefully. In his letter to Bosinney, Soames had written: 'You can spend up to £50 more than £12 000 if you have to.'. This was clear enough.

But Soames had also used the words 'a free hand'. The meaning of these three words was not very clear.

Perhaps the judge would say 'a free hand' meant that Bosinney could spend as much money as he liked. Soames knew that he had been less careful than usual when he had written these words. At the time, he had longed for the house to be finished. He had wanted to take Irene down to Robin Hill as soon as possible. Then there would be no reason for her ever to see Bosinney again.

Soames also wanted to make sure that Bosinney never built another house. Soames' hatred of Bosinney was like a madness. He was willing to do anything to ruin Bosinney.

One night at this time, Soames found Irene's door unlocked. He forced his way into her room and stayed the night. This action was a kind of madness too, for it could only make Irene hate her husband more than ever.

Soames was not happy about what he had done that night. The following morning, he still remembered the sound of Irene's crying. But he ate his breakfast and went to work as usual.

The weather that day was very bad and, by the afternoon, there was a thick fog all over London.

In the fog, it was difficult to hear any sounds. Men and women moved silently through the dark streets. Carriages moved slowly because their drivers found it almost impossible to see the road in front. People coughed in the thick air and held handkerchiefs to their faces. Their clothes were damp and the fog got into their eyes and noses.

People did not leave their homes unless they had to. If they had work to do, they tried to leave their shops or offices early. They wanted to get home before it was completely dark.

But, at about five o'clock, Dartie, Winifred's husband, left for his club as usual to eat and drink with his friends. Fog would not stop him from enjoying himself.

On the steps of his house, Dartie stopped for a moment, wondering whether to walk or to travel by Underground train. He decided to take the train and get out at Charing Cross, the nearest station to his club.

On the platform at Charing Cross, someone hurried past

Dartie. The man was hurrying so quickly that Dartie had to step back. The man was gazing straight in front with a strange, wild look in his eyes.

It was Bosinney, the Buccaneer. Dartie had not forgotten the evening he had spent at Richmond with Irene and Philip Bosinney. Dartie had wanted to drive home with Irene but Bosinney had stopped him. Dartie still remembered how angry he had been that night with Philip Bosinney.

Dartie's feeling of anger now returned. Bosinney looked like a man who was being hunted. Dartie decided to follow him. With a smile on his face, Dartie moved quickly after Philip Bosinney.

In his excitement, Dartie followed closely behind Bosinney. But just before he left the platform, Bosinney suddenly turned and rushed back to the train he had just left. He was too late. A porter held Bosinney back by his coat; the train was already moving out of the station.

Dartie looked quickly at the moving train and saw a woman dressed in grey fur sitting by a window. It was Soames' wife, Irene.

Dartie followed Bosinney more closely than ever – up the stairs, past the ticket-collector, into the street. At first, Dartie thought that Bosinney was drunk because he moved so quickly and so unsteadily. But Dartie soon saw that Bosinney was not drunk. Something had happened which was making Bosinney act like a madman.

Bosinney was talking to himself but Dartie could only hear the words 'Oh, God'. Bosinney did not seem to know where he was or where he was going.

Dartie almost felt sorry for Bosinney. He wondered what he and Irene had been talking about. Irene also had looked ill.

Dartie followed Bosinney through the fog as closely as he could. Dartie was a little worried by now. What was Bosinney planning to do? What had he and Irene been talking about?

Dartie followed Bosinney through the fog.

Was Bosinney going to throw himself under the wheels of a carriage?

At one moment, both men had to wait at the edge of the road. Dartie could hear what Bosinney was saying to himself now. Dartie understood what Soames had done the night before. The 'Man of Property' had forced his way into Irene's bedroom and stayed all night. That was why Bosinney, Irene's lover, seemed half-mad.

At last, the two men reached Trafalgar Square. Bosinney, very tired now, sat silently down on a seat and Dartie stood behind him, hidden by the fog.

Other men came close in the fog and passed by. They knew nothing of Bosinney's great unhappiness. Perhaps some of these men thought they had troubles of their own. But they had not received the great shock that Bosinney had.

Bosinney began to talk to himself again. Dartie wanted to touch Bosinney on the shoulder and speak to him. But Bosinney suddenly stood up and started walking again through the fog.

For the first time, Dartie became a little frightened.

'He can't go on long like this,' he thought. 'He's sure to be run over by a carriage.'

Dartie realized that Bosinney was now walking to the west.

'Perhaps he's going to fight Soames,' Dartie thought. This pleased him because he had never liked his cousin, Soames.

Dartie hurried on through the fog. Then someone shouted at him and he drew back. A carriage passed right in front of him. When it had gone, Dartie realized that he had lost Bosinney. He waited and listened for a few minutes, but there was no one there.

Dartie made his way to his club which was quite near and walked inside. Bosinney's strange behaviour in the fog had upset him, and he was quiet all evening.

———

That same evening, Soames Forsyte had left his office early because of the fog. He had been driven home very slowly and got back just before five o'clock. Irene's maid told Soames that his wife had gone out.

Why had Irene gone out in the fog? Soames could not understand it. He sat in front of the fire, trying to read the newspapers. But he could think only of Irene.

It was nearly seven o'clock when Soames heard Irene come in. It was then that he remembered what had happened the previous night. He remembered how she had cried, and he wondered what she would say to him now. Soames went out of the room to speak to Irene, but she was already on the stairs. She neither looked at Soames nor spoke to him. In her long, grey fur coat, she walked up the stairs like a complete stranger. She did not come downstairs again that night.

After he had eaten his dinner alone, Soames went to look at his pictures. They did not please him as much as usual. At last Soames went to bed, but it was a long time before he fell asleep.

15

Forsyte v. Bosinney

The court case of Forsyte *v.*[3] Bosinney was held the next day. The fog had gone and the sky was clear. Soames left the house that morning without seeing or speaking to his wife.

When Soames had first decided to bring the case against Bosinney he had been certain of the result. He was sure he must win the case. But then he began to talk to other men who knew about the law. Soames had used the words 'a free hand'. Bosinney had spent exactly what money he wanted to.

Perhaps the judge would say that Bosinney had been right to do this. But Soames had also said 'not more than another £50'. Surely this was clear enough? Bosinney had agreed to this, too.

Soames had spent a long time reading and re-reading his letters to Bosinney. The result of his case would depend on the meaning of two or three words. But the money was not important to Soames now. All he wanted was to ruin Philip Bosinney. If Soames won the case, Bosinney would not be able to go away with Irene. Neither of them would have any money. In this way, Soames thought he was making his property safe. He was also showing himself to be a good business man, a man who understood the law. Irene would stay with her husband and all this madness would be forgotten.

All these thoughts went through Soames' mind as he sat in the court that afternoon, waiting for his case to begin. He also thought back to the time before his marriage. He remembered how often he had asked Irene to be his wife and how often she had refused him. Soames had at last made a beautiful woman his property, but his marriage had been a complete failure. And now Soames was fighting to ruin his wife's lover.

Soames sat in the court thinking of all these things, but his face was completely calm. He never showed his feelings in public. No Forsyte ever did. Soames was, of course, neatly dressed. He looked exactly what he was – a clever solicitor, a gentleman, a Man of Property.

James, Soames' father, was in court to hear the case. He sat near the door so that he could leave quickly at the end. He had known that this young Bosinney would cause trouble.

James was secretly very proud of his son, who was sitting so calm and still in the middle of the court. James understood that the winning of the case was more important to Soames than the money. But he did not fully realize his son's hatred for Philip Bosinney. Such strong feelings were not thought correct for a Forsyte.

The judge now entered the court and the case began. There were quite a number of people in the court because the case was an interesting one. The meaning of two or three words might ruin a man's whole life. The result would be used in other cases and become part of the history of the courts.

Soames had paid for one of the best and most expensive barristers[3] to speak for him.

The barrister stood up and looked around the court.

'My client, Mr Soames Forsyte, is a gentleman ...' he began, 'a man of property ...'

The barrister told the court about the house at Robin Hill. He made it clear that Soames had spent a lot of money on the house. The architect, Mr Philip Bosinney, had ignored Mr Forsyte's instructions in his letters. And he had spent £350 more than the amount agreed to. It was this money that Mr Forsyte wanted the architect to pay back.

The barrister then asked Soames a few questions. Soames stood in the centre of the court, completely still. He answered the questions shortly, in a quiet, calm voice. Soames agreed that he had used the words 'a free hand', but he had also told Bosinney that he could spend no more than an extra £50.

James was pleased with his son. Soames' answers were short and yet very clear. Nobody could twist his words and give them a different meaning.

Bosinney's barrister now spoke, but he had very little to say. He wanted to ask Bosinney a few questions and his name was called through the court.

'Philip Bosinney ...' Three times the name was called. There was no answer. Bosinney was not in the building. James, for some reason, was a little afraid. He felt as though Bosinney would never come and would never answer to his name again.

The barrister then asked Soames a few questions.

The court sat in silence for a few minutes and then the judge began to speak. He read out again the letters Soames and Bosinney had written. He repeated all the answers that Soames had given to the court. At last, the judge gave his opinion. Soames had written that Bosinney had 'a free hand' in the spending of money. That was true. But Soames had also given an amount – £12 000 – and had said that Bosinney could spend only £50 more than this. Bosinney had spent £350 more. He was clearly in the wrong. The judge told the court that Philip Bosinney must pay this amount of money back to Soames.

James felt proud and happy. He left the court without waiting for Soames and drove straight home to tell his wife the result.

'Soames did very well,' James told his wife. 'He's a clever man and he answered well. But this won't please Old Jolyon. The Buccaneer, as they call Bosinney, will be ruined. Now, I wonder why he wasn't in court?'

James sat for a long time, looking at the fire, but he found no answer to his question. 'Bosinney wasn't in court – why?'

16

Message in the Jewel Box

Soames was feeling pleased as he left the court, but his face was as calm as ever. He knew now that Bosinney was a ruined man. He would build no more beautiful and unusual houses like Robin Hill. The Buccaneer would have to sell everything he owned to pay the money to Soames. He would never be able to marry.

As he walked home, Soames thought about what he would

say to Irene.

'Well, I've won my case,' he would say. 'It's finished. I don't want to be hard on Bosinney. He can have some time to pay. Now let's get away from London. We'll go down to the house at Robin Hill. We'll start our marriage again and forget what has happened.'

If Irene refused to be a good wife now, Soames thought, he would tell her he wanted a divorce[3]. That would frighten her. But perhaps Irene wanted a divorce. Perhaps she would go with Philip Bosinney after all.

Divorce. The word filled Soames with fear. He could not think clearly. If he had a divorce, everyone would know about it and there would be a scandal. He would have to sell the house at Robin Hill. Worst of all, he would perhaps never see Irene again.

With these thoughts in his mind, Soames hurried home to tell Irene the news about the case. Soames wondered what Irene would say. He wanted to see her, but he did not know what to say to her.

Irene's maid was in the hall when Soames opened the front door.

'Where is Mrs Forsyte?' Soames asked her.

'Mrs Forsyte left about three hours ago, sir. She took a large case and a bag with her.'

'What's that you said? What message did she leave?' Soames asked, trying to keep his voice quiet.

'Mrs Forsyte left no message, sir,' the maid replied.

Soames stared around him as though he didn't know where he was. Then he ran quickly up the stairs to Irene's room.

Everything was exactly as usual. Everything was in order. All Irene's things were still in her room. The servant must have made a mistake.

Soames sat on the bed and tried to think, but he could not. He got up and looked at himself in the mirror. His face was pale and tears had come into his eyes. He turned quickly, ran downstairs and out into the street. He felt a little calmer now and, as he hurried along, he began to think more clearly.

Soames made his way to Bosinney's rooms. Soames had to know if Irene was with her lover. But there was no light and the door was locked. Nobody answered his knocking.

Out in the street again, Soames took a cab to his father's house. On the way, he remembered about the jewels he had given to Irene. Irene had no money, but she could sell Soames' presents for hundreds of pounds. She would be able to live comfortably with Bosinney somewhere abroad. When Soames reached his father's house, he went straight upstairs. His parents were getting ready for dinner.

'Oh, Soames! Why have you come? We weren't expecting you,' James said. 'Aren't you well?'

Without thinking, Soames replied, 'I'm all right.'

James looked at his son more carefully. 'You don't look well.'

'Have you brought Irene with you?' Soames' mother asked.

'No,' Soames replied. 'She's ... she's left me.'

'Left you? What do you mean, left you?' repeated his father. 'You never told me she was going to leave you.'

'How could I tell you when I didn't know myself?' answered Soames angrily. 'What can I do now?'

'What can you do? You can go after her, of course,' said James, walking up and down the room.

'I don't know where she's gone,' Soames said.

'Don't know where she's gone?' said James. 'I know. She's gone after that young Bosinney, of course. I knew what would happen. There will be a scandal. That's what there will be.'

Soames agreed to stay to dinner. Other members of the family were there. When they asked him about Irene, he told them that she was ill. He could not tell them the truth yet.

Soames left his father's house at about ten o'clock and went home quickly. The house was in perfect order as before, but Irene was not there. Soames could not believe that Irene had really left him. He looked in her room for a message. Nearly every cupboard and every drawer was full of clothes just as usual. She seemed to have taken very little. Perhaps she had only gone away for a short holiday after all.

Soames came to the box where Irene kept all her jewels. He opened it and was surprised to see that it was not empty, as he had thought. All the things he had given her were there, even her watch. He noticed a small piece of paper, carefully folded. His name 'Soames Forsyte' was written on it. He opened it slowly.

'I think I have taken nothing that you or your family have given me,' it said. And that was all.

Soames looked at all the beautiful presents he had given his wife to make her love him. He understood now how much she hated him. He realized she had hated him for years. There was no hope now, he knew. Their marriage was over. Soames stood up slowly and carried the box into his own room.

17

Bosinney Disappears

What was June doing all this time? After a long holiday by the sea, she had returned to London with her grandfather. June was calmer now, but she had made up her mind to marry Philip Bosinney whether he loved her or not. June had known about the court case and had been in court to hear the result.

She went at once to Bosinney's rooms. She rang the bell, but there was no answer. Then June remembered that Bosinney kept a key to his rooms under the doormat. She found the key, unlocked the door and went into the room.

The small room was dirty and untidy. As she looked around, June saw that all the things that had belonged to Bosinney had gone. While she was looking sadly at a place where a painting had been, June felt someone standing behind her. She turned quickly. Irene was standing by the open door. June walked forward and in her friendly way held out her hand. Irene did not take it.

Then June's eyes became full of anger. With many jealous questions in her mind, June looked carefully at the woman who had once been her friend.

Irene was dressed in a long, grey fur coat and was wearing a grey fur hat. Under the hat, her face seemed as small as a child's. Her face was white and her eyes were dark and looked sad and tired. In her hand, Irene held a bunch of small flowers. Their strong scent filled the room. Irene looked at June without smiling.

'What have *you* come for?' June said. 'I came to tell Phil that he has lost the case.'

Irene still did not speak. She did not move. She seemed to be made of stone.

'What have you come for?' June asked again. Then, almost at once, she added, 'You have no right to be here.'

Irene answered, 'I have no right to be anywhere.'

'What do you mean?' June asked.

'I have left Soames. You often told me to.'

June put her hands over her ears. 'I don't want to hear. You have been a false friend to me. You've ruined my life and now you want to ruin Phil's.'

As June said these words, Irene turned quickly and hurried down the stairs, holding the flowers to her lips. June ran to the door and called out, 'Come back, Irene. Come back.'

The sound of her footsteps died away.

June did not know what to do. She waited some time for Bosinney to return and, when he did not, she made her way back to Old Jolyon's house in Stanhope Gate.

Old Jolyon, who had spent the afternoon with his son and his grandchildren, came home at six o'clock and spoke to June. He had decided that he would sell his great house and buy a smaller one in the country. He would live there with his son and his family. If June wanted to, she could come as well. Or she could live by herself with the money Old Jolyon would give her.

Old Jolyon told June all these things very carefully. He could see how unhappy she was.

'You will like your father,' he said. 'He's a kind, friendly man and the children are sweet little things.'

June said nothing at first. She had an idea of her own. Then she spoke.

'I think that's a fine idea,' she said. 'And if you buy a house in the country, why don't you buy the house at Robin Hill? It's finished now and I hear it's very beautiful. No one will live there now.'

'What about the 'Man of Property'? Isn't he going to live there?'

'No,' said June, 'I'm sure he is not.' But she would not tell Old Jolyon how she knew this.

'Have you seen young Bosinney?' Old Jolyon asked. Did the old man know the truth?

'No,' said June, 'I went to his rooms, but he wasn't there.'

Looking into his grand-daughter's face, Old Jolyon said, 'Do you know what they say about Bosinney and Irene?'

June suddenly became angry. 'Yes. No. I know … I don't know … I don't care!' she cried out.

Old Jolyon spoke again slowly. 'You want your own way in everything. I believe you would want him if he was dead.'

After a long silence, June said, 'You could buy the house at

Robin Hill. You needn't ask Soames. I know you don't like him. Go to Uncle James. And if you can't buy the house, please give Phil the money to pay Soames. Phil has no money at all, I know he hasn't.'

'Well, I'll think about it,' said Old Jolyon at last. He liked the idea of buying the house at Robin Hill. He could live there with his son, Young Jolyon. He had heard that it was a fine place, a house for a gentleman. He could take the house from that 'Man of Property', Soames Forsyte.

Old Jolyon knew that in the end he would do what June wanted. But he only said again, 'Well, I'll think about it.'

18

The Death of Philip Bosinney

At breakfast the next morning, June again spoke to Old Jolyon about the house. He agreed he would go and see his brother, James, and talk to him about it.

When Old Jolyon arrived at James' house, the two brothers shook hands and Old Jolyon immediately began to talk about the house at Robin Hill.

'I've come about that house and about young Bosinney,' he said. 'I hear he's lost his case. Now, if Soames doesn't want to live at Robin Hill because of all the trouble, I might buy the house myself. The price must be a fair one, of course. Soames has already lost money and I think he would be glad to sell it.'

James was surprised, but secretly pleased by what Old Jolyon said. He did not show his true feelings.

'Soames is here now if you would like to see him,' James said

'I'm not ready to see him yet,' said Old Jolyon quickly. He

got up and picked up his hat.

At that moment the door opened and Soames came in.

'There's a policeman here for Uncle Jolyon,' Soames said with a smile on his face.

Old Jolyon looked at Soames angrily.

'A policeman?' said James. 'I don't know anything about a policeman, but I suppose you had better see him, Jolyon.'

James and Soames left the policeman with Old Jolyon and walked out of the room.

'Well,' James said to Soames. 'I suppose we must wait and see what the policeman wants.'

'Your uncle came here to talk about the house at Robin Hill,' James added.

At the end of ten minutes, Old Jolyon came in. He raised his hand and spoke slowly.

'Young Bosinney has been run over by a carriage in the fog and killed. There's some talk of suicide,' he said.

James' mouth fell open. 'Suicide? What would he do that for? Why would Bosinney want to kill himself?'

'If your son doesn't know, who does?' Old Jolyon answered.

James was silent.

'He was killed at once,' Old Jolyon told his brother. 'It was yesterday in the fog. No one knew at first who he was. There were no papers in his pockets. I'm going to the hospital now; you and your son had better come too.'

———

Old Jolyon sent a message to his son. Young Jolyon arrived at the hospital soon after the others.

The four Forsytes stood together, looking down at the dead man. Soames left first, then James.

'Come to me soon, Jo,' said Old Jolyon to his son and he

too left the room where Bosinney's body lay.

Young Jolyon asked the policeman to tell him what had happened.

'I don't think it's suicide,' the policeman said. 'I'm sure it was an accident. Perhaps the young man was thinking of other things. This was in his pocket, sir.'

The policeman showed Young Jolyon a lady's handkerchief. The scent that Irene used came from it. It was the same handkerchief that Swithin had seen in Bosinney's hand at Robin Hill. Young Jolyon held it for a moment and then gave it back to the policeman.

'I'm afraid I don't know who the handkerchief belongs to,' said Young Jolyon. But the scent reminded him of the beautiful face of Irene. She was perhaps still waiting somewhere for Bosinney, her lover.

Young Jolyon looked down at Bosinney for the last time. It seemed to him that all the Forsytes were standing in the small room looking at the young man. This was more than the death of one man, thought Young Jolyon. Bosinney's death had been a kind of death for all the Forsytes. The Forsytes would never be the same again. This young man, Philip Bosinney, had changed the lives of all of them.

Young Jolyon walked slowly back to his father's house.

'Ah, Jo. You've come,' said Old Jolyon quietly when he saw his son. 'I've told little June. But someone ought to tell Irene. Will you go? It makes me sad to think of her waiting for him, all alone.'

19

'This is My House'

After he left the hospital, Soames walked quickly through the cold streets, but he had no idea where he was going.

He had heard nothing from Irene. Soames had told the servants that his wife had gone away for a short holiday.

At last Soames remembered where he was. He could not walk the streets for ever. He turned in the direction of his home.

Soames opened his front door quietly, as he usually did. He looked round the small hall, at the things of beauty he had bought for his home. Everything was the same. Then suddenly Soames noticed something. Irene's umbrella was on the hall table. So she had come back. Soames did not know whether to be glad or sorry. He hurried into the drawing-room. Irene was sitting by the fire in the darkness. She did not seem to see or hear anything.

'So you've come back?' Soames said. 'Why are you sitting there in the dark?'

Irene turned to look at her husband. She was still wearing her fur coat and hat. Her eyes were very big and dark and her face was completely white.

Soames understood at once. Irene knew that Bosinney was dead. She had come back to her husband's house because she had nowhere else to go. She was like an animal that has been caught and cannot run away. Soames was then certain that Bosinney had been his wife's lover. He suddenly wanted Irene to leave his house for ever.

They sat for a long time, looking at each other. Then Soames got up and went out of the house. He did not know what to think or what to do. Part of him wanted to let Irene go, to make her leave his house and never come back.

Then he thought, 'Now I can keep her. She has nowhere to go. She cannot leave me now.'

Soames walked round the square and at last came back to his own front door again. He saw that the door was open and that a man was standing there.

'What is it you want, sir?' Soames said sharply. The man turned. It was Young Jolyon.

'The door was open,' he said. 'Can I see your wife for a moment? I have a message for her.'

'My wife can see no one,' Soames answered.

He walked quickly past Young Jolyon and stood in front of him.

'She can see no one,' Soames said again.

There was a soft noise behind Soames as the drawing-room door opened. There stood Irene with her hands held out in front of her. There was a wild look of hope on her face and a light in her eyes. But when she saw who the two men were, the light left her face. Her hands dropped to her sides and she stood there like stone.

Soames turned round again to Young Jolyon. He saw the sad look in Young Jolyon's eyes and made an angry sound.

'This is my house,' Soames said, with a smile on his face. 'I don't need any help from you. I've told you once and I'll tell you again, I don't want you in this house.'

And Soames shut the door in Young Jolyon's face.

'My *wife* can see no one,' Soames answered.

Points For Understanding

1

1 What was the reason for the afternoon party at Old Jolyon's house?
2 Old Jolyon's house 'made his position in the world quite clear'. What was his position?
3 Why did the Forsytes give Bosinney the name 'The Buccaneer'?
4 June was going to marry Bosinney. What was Old Jolyon's attitude to this marriage and to Bosinney?

2

1 Why did June introduce Bosinney to Irene?
2 When June introduced Bosinney to Irene, what did she say to them both?
3 How were the following related to Old Jolyon?
   (a) James (b)Swithin (c) June (d) Soames
4 Why did Old Jolyon refer to Soames as 'the Man of Property'?
5 Why did the other Forsytes think the marriage between Irene and Soames was a sensible one?
6 What was Irene's attitude to her husband?

3

1 Why had Old Jolyon not seen his son for fourteen years?
2 Why did Old Jolyon not enjoy his dinner at the club?
3 Young Jolyon hesitated at first about entering his father's house. Why?
4 Why was it not necessary for the two men to arrange to meet again?
5 June was one of Old Jolyon's grandchildren. Who were the other two?

4

1 Soames thought of three reasons why it would be a good thing to move into the country. What were they?
2 Why did Soames think of choosing Bosinney as the man to build his house?
3 What was Soames' job in the City?
4 What persuaded Soames in the end to have his house built at the top of the hill?
5 What was Soames' opinion about the love between June and Bosinney? Did Irene agree?
6 Irene did not seem interested in the new house. At first, Soames was angry with her, then he decided to be content. Why?

5

1 Why were the Forystes particularly interested in Soames' idea of moving to the country?
2 What was the reason behind James' visit to his son and daughter-in-law?
3 James gave Irene some advice about Bosinney. What was the advice and how did Irene answer?
4 Why did Bosinney have less time to go out with June?
5 Did Bosinney's plans for the house please Soames?
6 How much extra money was the house going to cost?
7 Soames asked Irene if she thought Bosinney was good-looking. What was her reply?

6

1 What was worrying Soames about the house?
2 Bosinney told Soames: 'If you don't like my work, I'll leave at once.' What made Soames agree to keep Bosinney?
3 Who was Bosinney really building the house for?

7

1 June overheard Bosinney suggesting a meeting to Irene. Where and when did Bosinney suggest they should meet?
2 June asked Bosinney to take her to the house on Sunday. What was his reply? What do you think the engagement was?
3 'But June is a Forsyte,' Old Jolyon thought to himself. What did he mean by this?
4 Why did June sit by the open window in her room crying?

8

1 Bosinney brought a chair from the house for Swithin. What was Bosinney hoping would happen and why?
2 When Irene and Bosinney returned, what did Swithin notice in Bosinney's hand?
3 What words of Irene's did Swithin hear when the carriage was nearly overturned? What effect did they have on him?

9

1 Why did Irene and Bosinney's behaviour remind the Forsytes of Young Jolyon?
2 In his letter of May 15th, what complaints did Bosinney make to Soames?
3 In the same letter, Bosinney agreed to continue working for Soames on one condition. What was it?
4 Why did Soames want Old Jolyon to speak to Bosinney and did Old Jolyon agree?
5 In his letter of May 19th, Soames explained an expression that he had used in an earlier letter. What was the expression and how did Soames explain it?
6 Did Bosinney accept Soames' conditions?

10

1 What helped Old Jolyon to forget about his unhappiness?
2 Why did Young Jolyon not like to see the animals at the zoo?

3 Why did Old Jolyon suggest in anger that perhaps Young Jolyon
was on Bosinney's side?
4 Old Jolyon said that he did not believe that Irene and Bosinney
were in love. Was he telling the truth?

11

1 What did June hope might happen at the dance?
2 Why did June leave the dance so suddenly?
3 June and Old Jolyon left London. Where did they go and why?
4 Winifred suggested to Irene that they should go on an outing to
Richmond and that Irene should bring Bosinney. What was her
reason?
5 What made Bosinney threaten to knock Dartie over?
6 Why did Irene cry when Bosinney told her of his love?
7 In the last paragraph, the author uses the words 'the house where
Irene lived' rather than 'Irene's house'. What is suggested by this
choice of words?

12

1 Why was Young Jolyon not able to blame Bosinney?
2 'And *that* makes me different from most other Forsytes,' said
Young Jolyon. What was *that*?
3 'And a Forsyte likes his property,' Young Jolyon said to Bosinney.
What was he trying to tell Bosinney?

13

1 'Will you let me go?' Irene asked Soames. What was Soames'
reply?
2 What was the real reason for Soames' invitation to Bosinney to
come for dinner?
3 Why did Soames decide that Bosinney would have to pay £350?
4 The house at Robin Hill was completed, but Soames still had not
moved. Why not?
5 What action of Irene's showed Soames that she really hated him?

6 When he saw Irene and Bosinney together in the park, what did Young Jolyon think the future would be for Irene, Bosinney, June and Old Jolyon?
7 What would happen to Old Jolyon's money when he died?

14

1 What would happen to Bosinney if he lost the court case?
2 The meaning of three words which Soames had written to Bosinney was unclear. What were the words?
3 What was Soames' real reason for taking Bosinney to court?
4 What action of Soames' increased Irene's hatred of him?
5 How was Bosinney behaving when Dartie followed him?
6 Who did Dartie see in the train at Charing Cross?
7 Why was Irene's lover behaving so strangely?
8 Why did Dartie become a little frightened?
9 What troubled Soames that evening?

15

1 Why was the meaning of the three words 'a free hand' so important in the court case?
2 Which of the older Forsytes was in court?
3 Why were there many people in the court?
4 Why was Bosinney's barrister unable to ask Bosinney any questions?
5 What was the judge's decision?

16

1 In what ways did Soames think that Bosinney would be ruined?
2 Why did the possibility of divorce frighten Soames?
3 Why did Soames think at first that Irene would have enough money to live abroad with Bosinney?
4 What action of Irene's made Soames certain that his marriage was over?

17

1 When June returned to London, she was determined to do one thing. What was it?
2 Irene said to June, 'I have no right to be anywhere.' What did she mean?
3 When Old Jolyon told June that he was thinking of buying a house in the country, what suggestion did June make?
4 Would Old Jolyon agree to June's suggestion?

18

1 Why did Old Jolyon visit James?
2 James asked, 'Why would Bosinney want to kill himself?' Old Jolyon answered, 'If your son doesn't know, who does?' What did Old Jolyon mean by these words?

19

1 Why had Irene returned to Soames' house?
2 When Irene heard two men's voices at the door, a wild look of hope came to her face for a moment. What had she thought?
3 'And Soames shut the door in Young Jolyon's face.' What does this suggest about Soames' decision to make Irene go or let her stay?

Glossary

SECTION 1
Terms to do with polite society

cab (page 21)
>   see *carriage* below.

carriage (page 11)
>   every gentleman in polite society owned horses and a carriage.
>   In Chapter 3, Old Jolyon goes out to his club in his own
>   carriage, which he then sends home. Later, when he goes on to
>   the opera, he takes a cab. A cab was a small carriage pulled by a
>   horse which was used like a taxi.

clothes – *fashionable clothes* (page 11)
>   clothes which polite society thought were smart and tasteful
>   (See *taste* on page 90).

club (page 20)
>   a meeting-place for the gentlemen of polite society. The clubs
>   were very respectable and only men of polite society could
>   become members. Some famous London clubs of the nineteenth
>   century still exist in London. Their members all belong to the
>   upper- class of society.

conversation – *polite conversation* (page 12)
>   polite society had fixed ideas about the things which could be
>   spoken about when people met together.

down – *to settle down* (page 19)
>   men and women in polite society were expected to get married
>   when they were young, to buy a house and to have children.
>   This was known as settling down.

elegant (page 28)
>   graceful and expensive.

engagement – *to celebrate an engagement* (page 11)
>   when a man and woman agree to marry one another they
>   become engaged. The engagement usually takes place some time
>   before the wedding. A party is usually given to celebrate the
>   engagement.

engagement – *to have an engagement* (page 37)

> an engagement usually meant an arrangement to meet someone on business. It was also used to suggest an important promise to meet a friend.

governess (page 19)

> an educated woman employed by a wealthy family to look after the children and to educate them.

property – *the man of property* (page 16)

> someone who is rich and who owns many possessions. When Old Jolyon calls Soames 'the Man of Property', he is suggesting that Soames thinks of his wife as a piece of property.

property – *no respect for property* (page 12)

> Bosinney did not think that it was important to own property.

respectable (page 11)

> correct and appropriate behaviour in polite society is said to be respectable. A place is called respectable if it is a good place to live.

scandal (page 20)

> when someone does something which breaks the rules of polite society that person causes a scandal. People are shocked and upset by the way that person has behaved.

taste – *good taste* (page 11)

> today your 'taste' means what you like. But in the nineteenth century 'good taste' was decided by polite society. Society said what its members should like and what they should not like. What was 'good taste' was also respectable.

time – *correct amount of time* (page 18)

> a party in polite society lasted only for a short time. Then guests were expected to leave without being told.

SECTION 2
Terms to do with business and finance

agent (page 26)

> a person who acts for the owners in the buying and selling of land.

bargain (page 25)

> something that you buy for less than its true value.

bills (page 32)

lists of things which have been bought, showing the prices paid for them.

City – *the City* (page 25)

the part of London where many important banks and businesses have their main offices.

debt – *to be in debt* (page 21)

to owe money to people.

hand – *to have a free hand* (page 45)

to be allowed to do as you want.

ruin – *to ruin someone* (page 61)

to do something to someone so that they lose their business, their money and their possessions.

SECTION 3
Terms to do with English law

In England, criminals are taken to criminal courts. But there are two other courts known as civil courts and divorce courts. Civil courts usually decide arguments about money and property. Divorce courts decide whether a marriage between husband and wife is to be ended or not.

barrister (page 69)

anyone who brings a case to court has to hire someone to speak for them. This person is trained in law and is called a barrister. The person who hires the barrister is called the client.

case (page 62)

a matter brought before a court for a decision.

divorce (page 72)

in nineteenth century England, there was only one way to end a marriage. One of the partners had to go to a divorce court and accuse the other partner of doing something wrong. A divorce in polite society was always a big scandal. (See *scandal* on page 90.)

In the matter of Soames and Irene, Soames had done nothing wrong. Irene could not take him to court. Irene had done something wrong. She and Bosinney were lovers. But, if Soames did not take her to court, there could be no divorce.

v. – *Forsyte v. Bosinney* (page 67)

v. is a shortened form of *versus* – the Latin word for 'against'. The whole phrase means the case of Forsyte against Bosinney.

will – *changed his will* (page 62)

a will is a paper which says what a person wants done with their property after their death. A person changes their will by altering what they have written on this paper.

SECTION 4

Terms to do with character and emotion

confident (page 12)

feeling strong and sure of yourself. The Forsytes felt confident because they were all together as a family.

feelings – *a hard man with no feelings* (page 48)

a cruel unkind man.

mean (page 60)

unwilling to let anyone take things which belong to you, usually money.

patience – *to have no patience* (page 19)

to become easily angry or annoyed. Old Jolyon easily became angry with those members of his family that he did not like.

pity (page 22)

feelings of sadness. You feel pity for someone if you are sorry about their troubles.

stern (page 24)

with no feelings of kindness.

stone – *made of stone* (page 60)

if you describe someone as made of stone, you mean that they are cold and unkind.

stubborn (page 15)

refusing to change your mind after you have decided something.

JOHN GALSWORTHY

(unsimplified)

Villa Rubein, and Other
  Stories, 1898
The Island Pharisees
The Man of Property
The Country House
Fraternity
The Patrician
The Dark Flower
The Freelands
Beyond
Five Tales
Saint's Progress
In Chancery
To Let
The White Monkey
The Silver Spoon
Swan Song
On Forsyte Change
Maid in Waiting
Flowering Wilderness
Over the River

The Forsyte Saga
Caravan
A Modern Comedy
End of the Chapter

A Commentary
A Motley
The Inn of Tranquillity
The Little Man, and Other
  Satires
A Sheaf
Another Sheaf
Tatterdemalion
The Burning Spear
Captures
Castles in Spain
Two Forsyte Interludes

Moods, Songs, and Doggerels
Verses New and Old

Addresses in America

Memories. *Illustrated by Maud
  Earl*
Awakening. *Illustrated by R. H.
  Sauter*

The Forsyte Saga. *Illustrated by
  Anthony Gross*

Plays: *Eight Vols.*
Complete Plays: *One Vol.*

UPPER LEVEL

Great Expectations *by Charles Dickens*
Bleak House *by Charles Dickens*
Of Mice and Men *by John Steinbeck*
The Great Ponds *by Elechi Amadi*
Rebecca *by Daphne du Maurier*
Our Mutual Friend *by Charles Dickens*
The Grapes of Wrath *by John Steinbeck*
The Return of the Native *by Thomas Hardy*
Weep Not, Child *by Ngugi wa Thiong'o*
Precious Bane *by Mary Webb*
Mine Boy *by Peter Abrahams*
The Cut-glass Bowl and Other Stories *by F. Scott Fitzgerald*

For further information on the full selection of Readers
at all five levels in the series, please refer to the
Heinemann Readers catalogue.

Heinemann English Language Teaching
A division of Heinemann Publishers (Oxford) Ltd
Halley Court, Jordan Hill, Oxford OX2 8EJ

OXFORD   MADRID   ATHENS   PARIS   FLORENCE   PRAGUE
SÃO PAULO   CHICAGO   MELBOURNE   AUCKLAND
SINGAPORE   TOKYO   IBADAN   GABORONE
JOHANNESBURG   PORTSMOUTH (NH)

ISBN 0 435 27270 5

This retold version by Margaret Tarner for Heinemann Guided Readers
Text © Heinemann Publishers (Oxford) Ltd 1995
Design and illustration © Heinemann Publishers (Oxford) Ltd 1995
First published 1975
This edition 1995

Illustrated by Nick Hardcastle
Typography by Adrian Hodgkins
Designed by Sue Vaudin
Cover by Haydn Cornner and Marketplace Design
Typeset in 10.5/12.5 pt Goudy
Printed and bound in Malta by Interprint Limited

95 96 97 98 99 10 9 8 7 6 5 4 3 2 1